His Royal Buckliness

To Ken, Jen, and the Adventure Men

Library of Congress Cataloging in Publication Data   Hawkes, Kevin. His Royal Buckliness / by Kevin Hawkes.   p.   cm.   Summary: Carried off to a frozen land by the giants to be their king, Lord Buckley misses the delights of summer and spring. ISBN 0-688-11062-2. — ISBN 0-688-11063-0 (lib. bdg.) [1. Giants—Fiction. 2. Seasons—Fiction. 3. Stories in rhyme.] I. Title. PZ8.3.H288Hi 1992 [E]—dc20   91-40347 CIP AC

His Royal Buckliness

Kevin Hawkes

LOTHROP, LEE & SHEPARD BOOKS   NEW YORK

The giants stole Lord Buckley and crowned him their king, then carried him to their frozen land filled with giant things.

They washed his ears, combed his hair, dressed him warmly,
  fed him cake,

but wouldn't let him slide or bump or run for fear he'd break.
This made his Royal Buckliness feel all alone and cranky!

So he wrote to southern cousins, and sealed the bottle tight,
and hurled it into ocean waves beneath the pale moonlight,

where it tossed and drifted for weeks and months and more...

...until at last, in a warmer place,

it gently washed ashore.

Then over the sea Sir Joshua came,
and with him came Sir Jake,

to find his Royal Buckliness beside the frozen lake.

Through sparkling snow,

on raven's wing,

past campfires all a-smoking,

they traveled north to bring their friend

a bag of bullfrogs croaking!

Signs of summer, songs of spring,

made those giant hearts take wing!

And in the end, they parted friends,

and sent Lord Buckley home again.